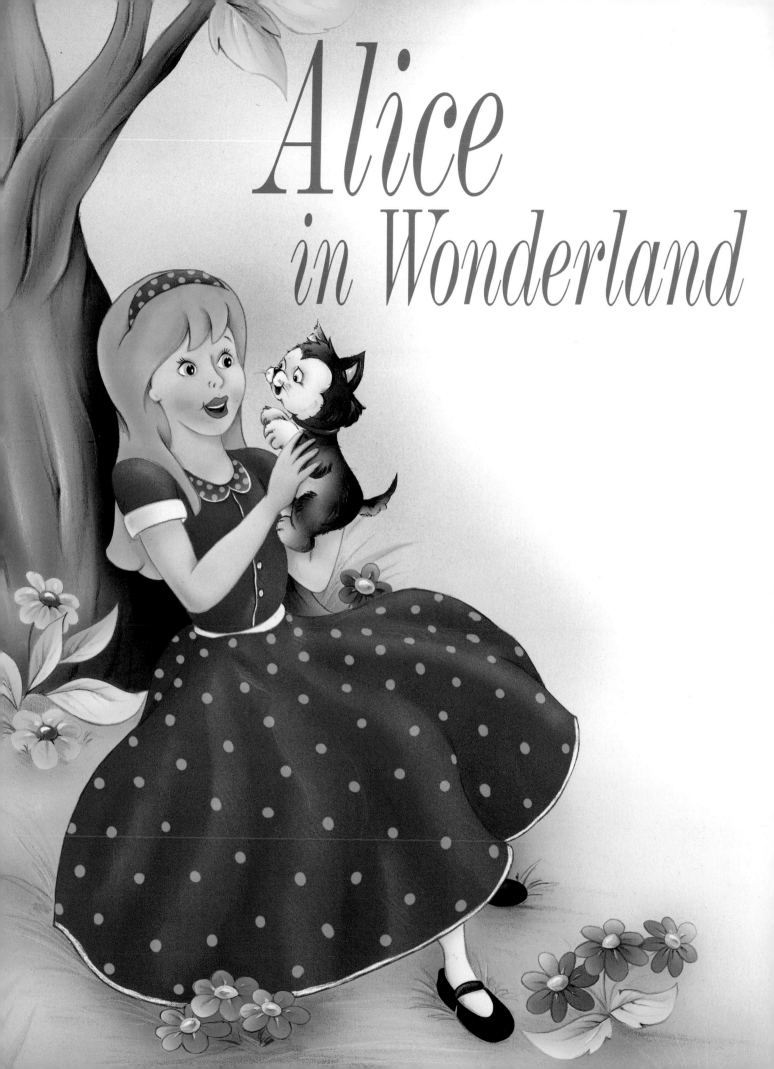

Alice in Wonderland

One day, after a long walk in the countryside, Alice, while her sister was off picking flowers, lay down at the foot of a tree and dozed off.

As she was dozing, a white rabbit ran by at full speed, muttering, 'I'll be late!'

Alice woke with a start, amazed not just that the rabbit could talk, but also that he was elegantly dressed and had a watch. 'He looks terribly busy!' the girl thought.

At a certain spot, as smiling flowers said hello, the rabbit stopped and ducked into a hole in the ground.

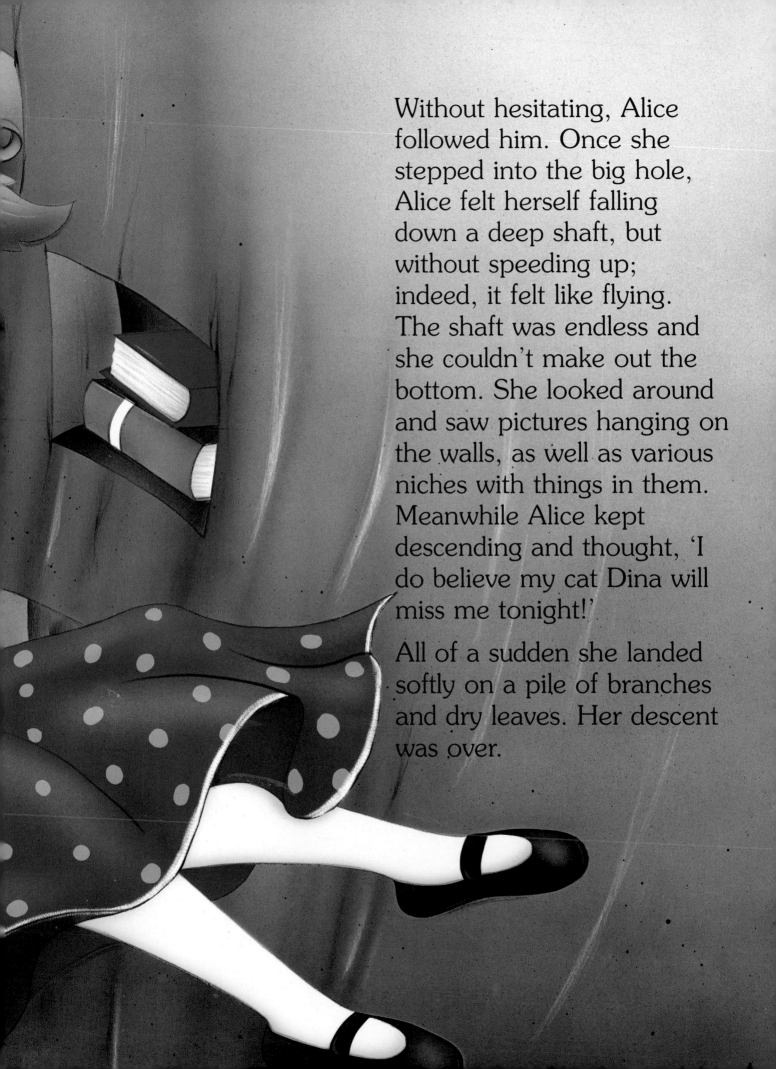

Without hesitating, Alice followed him. Once she stepped into the big hole, Alice felt herself falling down a deep shaft, but without speeding up; indeed, it felt like flying. The shaft was endless and she couldn't make out the bottom. She looked around and saw pictures hanging on the walls, as well as various niches with things in them. Meanwhile Alice kept descending and thought, 'I do believe my cat Dina will miss me tonight!'

All of a sudden she landed softly on a pile of branches and dry leaves. Her descent was over.

She found herself in the middle of a large room with many doors. She tried opening one, but it told her, 'You can't come in, you're too big!'

On top of a table she saw, next to a gold key, a little bottle labelled 'DRINK ME'. Alice checked that it didn't say 'Poison' elsewhere on the bottle and then drank it in one gulp.

'What good syrup this is!' thought Alice. Then she realised she had shrunk to the size of a mouse.

'Oh no, I left the key on the table! Now how will I get it?'

On the floor, she spotted a box of biscuits labelled 'EAT ME'. She tried one and began to grow so fast that her head almost hit the ceiling. At that height poor Alice certainly couldn't get through the door!

She sat down and began to cry, gushing tears by the litre.

A moment later the White Rabbit went by. Alarmed, he dropped a fan before making off at high speed. Alice picked it up and began fanning herself, and guess what? To her astonishment she shrank back down. She soon realised that it was the fan she was holding in her hand that had made her shrink again, and quickly dropped it so she didn't run the risk of disappearing completely.

Meanwhile, her foot had slipped and she was sitting in the water. She realised that she was in a puddle of the tears that she had shed when she was big. 'So now what will I do?'

It wasn't long before she heard the sound of distant footsteps.

She got up out of the puddle and headed in the direction of the noise.

She ended up in front of a pretty little cottage.

The White Rabbit was leaning out the window, shouting, 'Marianne, the gloves, the fan… I can't keep the duchess waiting!'

Alice realised that the rabbit had mistaken her for his housemaid. She went inside to look for the gloves, but saw a little flask. She took a sip and started growing and growing.

'What's happening to me?' cried Alice. The house had become too small for her. She was trapped!

The White Rabbit was annoyed. He was waiting for the gloves and the fan, but they didn't arrive. Hearing a mighty racket, he whipped around and saw that Alice was trapped.

The situation wasn't good. Then Alice heard: 'A handful will do!' and felt cupcakes hitting her face. Alice ate one and immediately started shrinking again. As soon as she was small enough to fit through the door she left the cottage and headed for the nearby forest.

Alice saw an enormous toadstool on which there lay a big, fat, sleepy-looking green caterpillar, smoking calmly. 'And who might you be?' he asked in a drowsy voice.

'I don't even know myself any more! Since this morning I've kept changing size. I want to be big again,' sighed Alice.

'One side of the toadstool will make you grow; the other will make you shrink. Help yourself,' the caterpillar said, crawling away.

Alice broke off two pieces of toadstool and nibbled on one. Luckily it was from the right side and she went back to normal size.

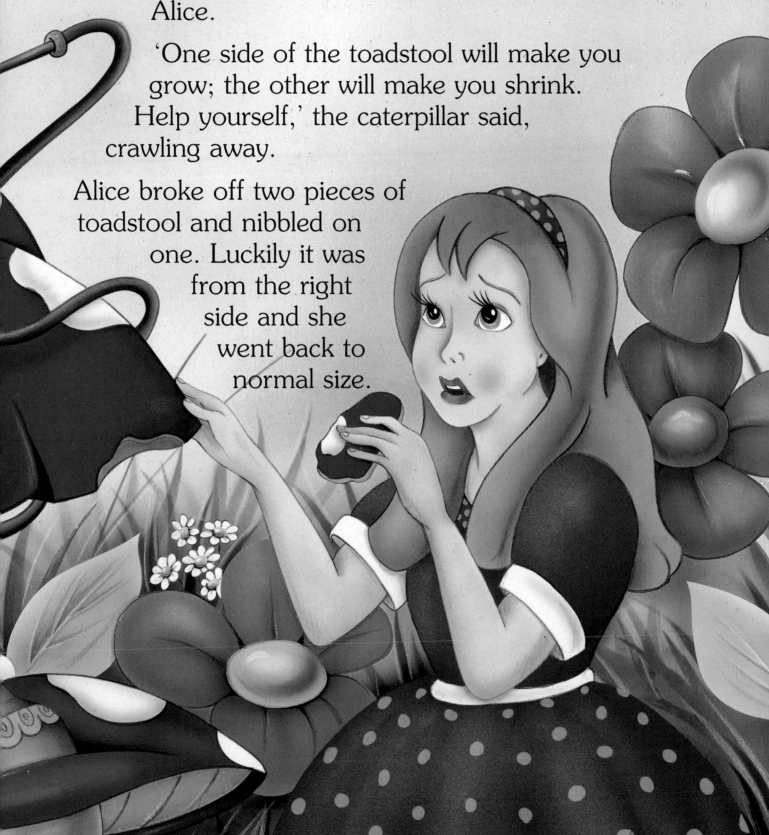

A moment later she noticed a cat curled up on the branch of a tree.

'Hello,' she said, surprised. 'Who are you?'

'I'm the Cheshire Cat,' the animal replied, grinning.

'Mr Cat, which way should I go to get out of here?' Alice asked.

'Whichever direction you take will be the right one,' the cat replied with a wide smile.

'There,' the cat lifted his left paw and pointed, 'lives the Mad Hatter and, on the other side, the March Hare. Go and see whichever one you like, they're quite mad!' And with that he vanished.

Alice was getting so used to strange things happening in this peculiar land that she wasn't surprised when the cat suddenly vanished. She set off again, and it wasn't long before she came upon a house with chimneys in the shape of long ears. It was the March Hare's house. Alice took a bite of the remaining piece of toadstool and shrank enough to go inside.

The March Hare was having tea with the Mad Hatter and the dormouse, who was having a nap.

'Please, have some wine!' said the Hatter to Alice.

'I don't drink wine!' she exclaimed.

'Actually, there isn't any,' replied the Hatter.

Alice thought, 'They really are mad!' and slipped away.

Cautiously she headed into the forest, where she saw an enormous rosebush full of white flowers. Some gardening elves were painting them red and muttering, 'We were meant to plant red roses here, not white ones! If the Queen of Hearts finds out she'll have our heads!'

As soon as they saw Alice they ran off.

The girl took a paintbrush and a tin of paint and began colouring in the flowers.

A short time later she heard: 'The Queen is coming!'

The royal procession stopped right in front of Alice.

The courtiers had uniforms decorated with symbols and flat bodies to which their arms and legs attached.

'What is your name?' demanded the Queen of Hearts.

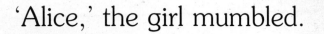

'Alice,' the girl mumbled.

'Off with her head!' ordered the Queen.

'That's ridiculous!' said Alice firmly.

The Queen of Hearts was speechless at this impertinence. Then she exclaimed angrily, 'Prepare for trial!'

They all went off to court. Alice had never been at a trial before, but she had read lots of books. She recognised the White Rabbit, who was holding a scroll of parchment in his hand.

The Queen ordered: 'Proceed with the charges!'

The White Rabbit unrolled the scroll and began reading. 'First we will hear the testimony...'

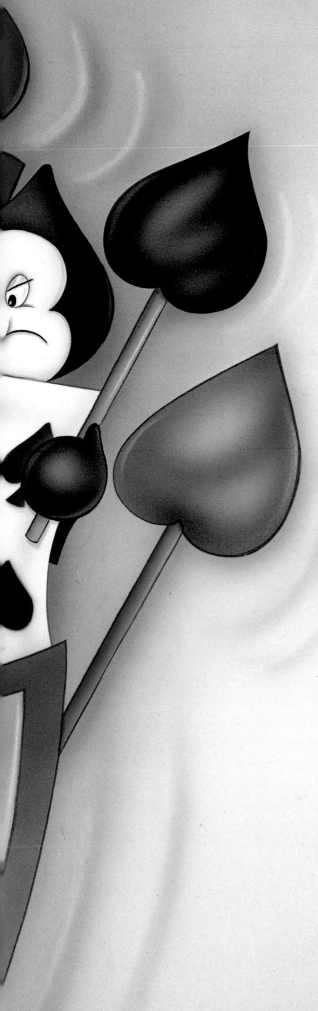

But the Queen of Hearts exploded with rage. 'The jurors are to issue a guilty verdict immediately!'

Chaos reigned in the courtroom and there was much shouting.

Filled with indignation at a trial where she didn't even know what she'd been accused of, Alice jumped to her feet. 'What nonsense!' she exclaimed.

The Queen ordered: 'Off with her head!'

The guards rushed towards Alice who, in the meantime, was returning to normal size. 'But who's to say I should obey you? You're no more than a pack of cards!' she exclaimed.

With this the cards scattered, falling onto Alice who, panicking slightly, tried to get them off her.

She needn't have bothered, as her sister was already busy picking off the leaves that had fallen from the tree. Indeed, it was these leaves which Alice, having arrived at the end of her amazing dream, had mistaken in her sleep for playing cards.

'What a good sleep you've had,' her sister was saying.

Alice sat up, rubbing her eyes, and found herself under the tree in the middle of the countryside. She began telling her sister about all the extraordinary characters she'd met in the strange wonderland. And who knows: maybe there really is a White Rabbit…